Nicholas and the Rocking Horse

A first horse for Nicholas Kennedy
J.R.

For Trisha and Graham with love
I.D.

First published in the United States by
Ideals Publishing Corporation
Nashville, Tennessee 37214
First published in Great Britain by
J.M. Dent & Sons, Ltd
London, England

Library of Congress Cataloging-in-Publication Data

Richardson, Jean.
    Nicholas and the rocking horse/by Jean Richardson: illustrated
by Ian Deuchar.
      p. cm.
    Summary: A little boy rents a rocking horse for a year and a day
during which he is taken on five magical rides.
    ISBN 0-8249-8481-1
    [1. Horses—Fiction. 2. Toys—Fiction. 3. Magic—Fiction.]
  I. Deuchar, Ian, ill. II. Title
PZ7.R39485N1 1990
[E]—dc20   90-4448
                                         CIP

Printed in Italy   AC

The illustrations in this book were prepared in
watercolor on Arches paper.

NICHOLAS
AND THE ROCKING HORSE

By Jean Richardson   Illustrated by Ian Deuchar

IDEALS CHILDREN'S BOOKS
Nashville, Tennessee

The moment Nicholas saw the rocking horse in the antique shop, he wanted it more than anything else in the world.

He could see that it was old. Although its dappled paint had faded, it still had most of its mane and tail. And Nicholas was sure that his father could fix the broken leather reins.

His mother was busy looking at some old china, so Nicholas asked the price of the horse. He was very disappointed when the woman said firmly, "The horse is not for sale."

"Then why is it in the window?" Nicholas asked, trying not to cry.

"The horse is not for sale," the woman repeated, "but you can rent it. How much can you afford?"

Nicholas pulled out his pockets. He had several shells, his favorite marble, a whistle, and a miniature battleship.

"I have some money at home," he said. "You can have everything in my piggy bank."

"That won't be necessary," the woman said, taking the marble with the frozen pattern inside. "This will buy you a year and a day, and five rides."

Nicholas was so excited that he didn't argue about five rides. Silly woman! Once he had the horse at home, he could have as many rides as he liked.

The horse stood in the corner of Nicholas's room near the window.

At first Nicholas was content to rock gently back and forth, but the horse seemed impatient; and Nicholas felt that it longed to stride out and let the wind comb its mane.

One evening it began to rock so hard that Nicholas had to hold on tight. He remembered a game he used to play with his mother . . .

This is the way,
This is the way the soldier rides,
When he goes to salute the Queen . . .

A strap pressed against his chin and Nicholas saw he was wearing a scarlet jacket and a gleaming breastplate. He guessed that he had on a plumed helmet like the other guards ahead of him.

The route to the palace was lined with cheering crowds. As he rode proudly along, Nicholas longed to see someone he knew.

Suddenly, in the sea of faces, he thought he saw his mother. But would she recognize him?

Nicholas was so excited that he couldn't resist waving. Now she would know that it was he.

Just as he thought she had seen him, the crowds and the troop of horses vanished in a sudden swirl of mist . . .

After that, Nicholas often pretended to be a guardsman, but although he sat up very straight and kept repeating, *"This is the way the soldier rides,"* the rocking horse didn't take any notice.

Several weeks later, he caught a bad cold. He was lying in bed when suddenly the horse seemed to summon him. As Nicholas climbed on its back, he became dizzy and a voice said:

This is the way,
This is the way the acrobat rides,
When he does his most daring trick.

The next moment, to his astonishment, he was swinging on a trapeze high above a circus ring. When he dared to look down, he saw a horse circling at top speed.

"Ladies and gentlemen!" boomed the ringmaster, cracking his whip with a noise like gunfire. "The Great Nicholoff will now do a triple somersault from the bar and land on the horse's back."

As Nicholas swung out over the audience, the tense silence was broken only by the jingling bells on the horse's harness.

He took a deep breath, let go of the bar, and found himself tumbling through the air . . .

Nicholas thought he heard the horse say, "Gotcha!" as he landed. They pranced around the ring to a storm of applause. The audience wanted an encore, but their shouts turned into the creaking of the rockers.

When he went back to school, Nicholas was better at somersaults than anyone else.

One evening after he'd been naughty, his father carried Nicholas upstairs and said, "Go straight to bed" very firmly.

As Nicholas lay in bed feeling very sorry for himself, he felt the horse calling him. It bucked furiously beneath him as a voice whispered:

This is the way,
This is the way the highwayman rides,
When he flies through the night to a holdup.

Nicholas was wearing a mask and a jaunty three-cornered hat. A long cloak as black as mischief streamed out behind him as the wind buffeted his face. He was galloping like a madman through the darkness to hold up a coach at the crossroads.

When it came into sight. Nicholas reined in his horse and called out boldly: "Stand and deliver!"

"Spare my life, sir," begged the trembling coachman, offering Nicholas his money and his watch.

But the passenger was not so easily frightened. She looked calmly at Nicholas with eyes as blue as his mother's, and she was the prettiest girl he'd ever seen. He knew he couldn't possibly take anything from her . . .

Being a highwayman was so real that when he woke up the next morning, Nicholas was sure that it wasn't just a dream. He decided it must have something to do with the five rides mentioned by the woman in the shop. If so, he had already used three of them.

He wondered if for once the horse would let him choose the ride.

As though it could read his mind, the horse began to rock faster and faster. Nicholas could almost see the wood melting into slender legs that bunched forward into a headlong gallop. He smiled as he heard the familiar words:

This is the way,
This is the way the jockey rides,
When he wants to win a race . . .

Nicholas crouched on the neck of the horse, standing in his stirrups. With hooves drumming the hard ground like thunder, the horse jostled its way to the front of the runners.

The white rails flashed past. Nicholas heard the roar of the crowds.

There were other riders at his shoulder. Their horses were neck and neck. All his willpower and determination flowed into the horse as the finish came in sight. On and on they raced. Was the horse beside him winning?

Nicholas felt as one with the horse as it threw itself forward and . . .

"Did we do it?" he cried, not sure if they had won — but once again he was back in his bedroom.

Nicholas guessed that the horse would make the last ride something very special. He didn't want it to happen, not yet; and he tried not to remember that soon the year and a day would be up.

One evening when it was already dark outside and Nicholas was playing with his toys, the horse began to rock all by itself. Nicholas realized that he hadn't ridden it for some time.

"I still love you," he said, stroking its mane as he rocked gently to and fro, and he thought he heard the horse reply:

This is the way,
This is the way that Pegasus flies
As we soar through time and space.

Tossing its head, the rocking horse leaped through the window, and they flew out into the night.

They galloped across plains of clouds under a canopy of stars — it was the longest ride so far. The moon was a silvery-gold disk that paled as the sun appeared on the horizon.

Now the clouds turned pale pink. Nicholas broke off a piece and it tasted of raspberry. He felt full of energy and was sure that he could do anything: run, jump, climb, swim, ride a bicycle, read, write, even grow taller.

And someone — was it Pegasus? — seemed to be telling him that everything was possible now that he had learned to ride the magic horse of his imagination.

Nicholas didn't remember how or when they got back, but he fell asleep to the sound of the horse gently rocking in its corner.

When he woke up, the room was bright with moonlight. He knew at once that something had happened: the horse was gone.

It left no mark behind, not even a dent in the carpet, but through his tears Nicholas saw something that glinted like a star. When he looked closer, it was only a marble, but it was the marble he had given the woman in the antique shop. A year and a day ago.

The next time Nicholas and his mom went shopping and passed the antique shop, there was the horse in the window. Nicholas knew that it was the same horse.

A boy who looked younger than Nicholas was looking at it, and Nicholas could tell that the boy wanted the horse more than anything else in the world.

You can't have it, it's mine, he thought indignantly.

But even as he thought this, Nicholas knew that he was too old for a rocking horse.

What he really wanted — and he was sure Pegasus wouldn't mind — was a bike, a bike on which he could have all sorts of new adventures with his friends.

When he looked back, the boy had gone into the shop. Nicholas waved good-bye to Pegasus and was almost sure he saw his head dip forward in a gentle return salute.